DATE DUE

M Scout			
MDH 99			
M			
GAYLORD			PRINTED IN U.S.A.

Max's Wacky Taxi Day

MAX GROVER

BROWNDEER PRESS   **HARCOURT BRACE & COMPANY**   San Diego   New York   London

Browndeer Press is a registered trademark
of Harcourt Brace & Company.

Library of Congress Cataloging-in-Publication Data
Grover, Max
Max's wacky taxi day/Max Grover
p.   cm.
"Browndeer Press"
Summary: Visual and verbal puns punctuate the
story of Max's day as a taxicab driver delivering
passengers around the city.
ISBN 0-15-200989-2
[1. Taxicab drivers—Fiction.   2. Puns and punning—
Fiction.]
I. Title.
PZ7.G93113Max   1997
[E]—dc20   96-2333

First edition
F E D C B A

Printed in Singapore

for MOM and DAD

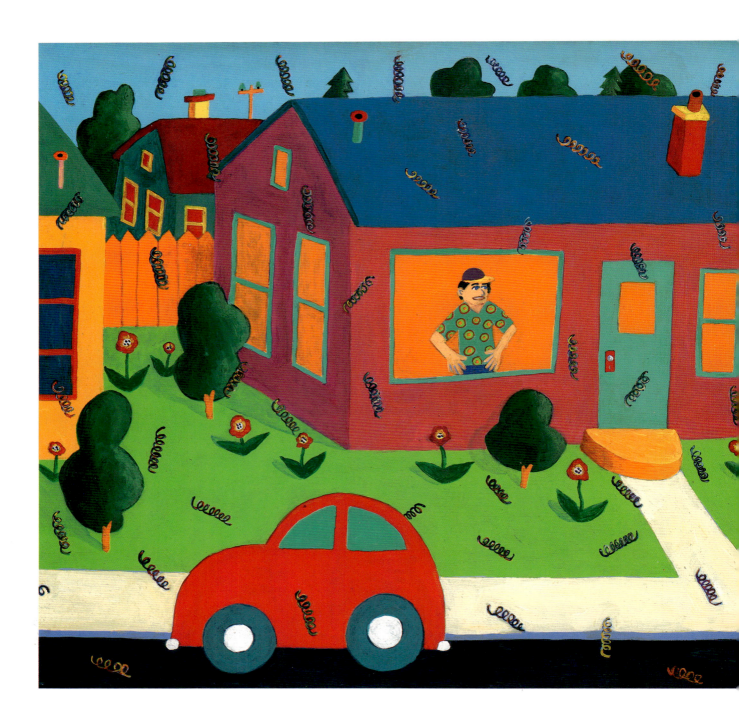

One morning Max the taxi driver hopped out of bed to greet the day. "I hope it doesn't rain," he said. But when he looked out the window, he noticed some **SPRING SHOWERS**.

His first customer, Ms. Wing, was a pilot on her way to work. "Please take me out to the **AIRPLANE HANGER**," she said.

Max replied, "It's very foggy this morning and no planes can fly. The radio said the airport is **ALL SOCKED IN**!"

After leaving the airport, Max picked up Mr. Carpenter, who wanted to take his son to the playground. Max drove along the beach. "Just take a look at that **SEA SAW**," he said.

Mr. Carpenter was impressed. "That ship carries some heavy cargo," said Max. "I hope it won't **SINK THE BOAT**."

**Max's next passengers were Marina and her mom.
"I just lost a tooth," Marina said, "and we were on
our way to the dentist."**

"Why not take the **TOOTH FERRY**?" asked Max.
He dropped them off at the dock.

Miss Sacks climbed into Max's taxi. "I've been shopping for an hour and I need to rest," she said. "Here's a good spot," said Max, and he stopped in front of the PARK BENCH.

Ms. Hastings got into Max's taxi. "I'll be late for my meeting, and I wish I could let them know," she said. "I guess I need a CAR PHONE," said Max. "Everyone else seems to have one."

Max dropped off Ms. Hastings and drove for a while, wondering whether to go left or right. He couldn't decide until he came to a FORK IN THE ROAD.

Reggie and Paige stepped into Max's taxi. They were on their way to today's game.

"Let's look at some BASEBALL DIAMONDS on the way to the ballpark," Max said.

Traffic was getting heavier and heavier, and Max was driving slower and slower. He said to himself, "I need a break. I'd better stop for some lunch and **MUSICAL CHAIRS.**"

After lunch Max was thirsty. I could use a soda, he thought. Then he saw a parade. "Perfect!" he said. "Here comes the STRAWBERRY FLOAT."

A little later Max's taxi slowed to a crawl again. All around him cars and buses had stopped, too. There must be a TRAFFIC JAM up ahead, thought Max.

Ms. Twigg got into Max's taxi. "Someone spilled a barrel of honey in the middle of the street," she said. "I've never seen such a **STICKY MESS**."

"I see the problem," Max replied. "A car is stuck.
It's a good thing the **BIG TOE TRUCK** came quickly."

The Fields family got into Max's taxi. "Our TV set is broken and we can't watch the football game. What shall we do?" asked Mrs. Fields.

"I know!" Max said. "Why not go **BOWLING**?"

Rod and Bob hailed Max and his taxi. They were on their way to do some fishing. "I know a good spot," said Max. "Let me take you to the CREEK IN THE STAIRS."

Next Maurice and his dog, Hector, climbed into the taxi. Hector wouldn't stop barking. "I need to take you where you can TRAIN YOUR PET," said Max.

Max's wacky day was coming to an end. His friend Cliff got into Max's taxi and said, "I've got a ticket to the ROCK CONCERT. How about a lift?"

It was dark as Max left the concert. "Time to quit," he said. "I'm hungry." He went home and started to **FIX DINNER**.

After dinner Max read a book and then went to bed. As he turned out the light, he said to himself, "This was a pretty FAIR DAY after all." He closed his eyes and dreamed all about it.

The illustrations in this book were done in acrylics
on D'Arches Lavis Fedilis drawing paper.
The display type was set in Futura Light, Futura Book, Futura Bold,
and Futura Extra Bold. The text type was set in Futura Extra Bold.
Color separations by Bright Arts, Ltd., Singapore
Printed and bound by Tien Wah Press, Singapore
This book was printed on totally chlorine-free Nymolla Matte Art paper.
Production supervision by Stanley Redfern and Ginger Boyer
Designed by Camilla Filancia